I0760684

BLACK HOLE ECHOES

COSMIC TALES OF THE UNKNOWN

WRITTEN BY: ODDNESS

ART BY: MIKE DUBISCH

BLACK HOLE ECHOES
SECOND EDITION 2024
ODDNESS

HARDBACK ISBN: 978-1-960213-33-4
ELECTRONIC ISBN: 978-1-960213-34-1

ALL ARTWORK BY MIKE DUBISCH
WORDS, LAYOUT, AND EDIT BY ODDNESS

ORDERING INFORMATION:
INFO@ODDNESS.US

WWW.ODDNESS.US

BLACK HOLE ECHOES

COSMIC TALES OF THE UNKNOWN

WRITTEN BY: ODDNESS

ART BY: MIKE DUBISCH

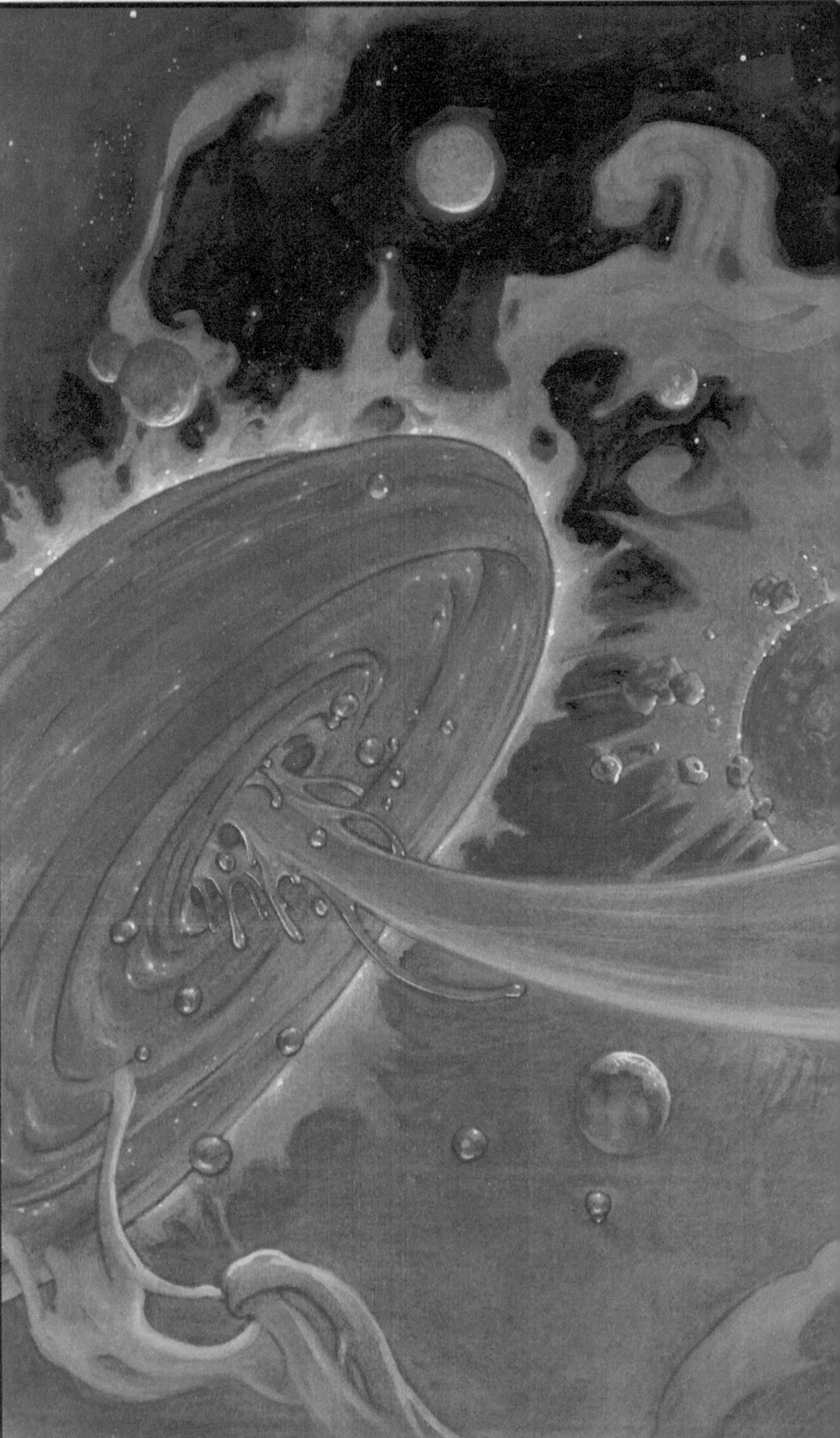

CONTENTS

INTERLUDE ONE 1-8

THE STAR FARMER ... 9-19

INTERLUDE TWO 20-21

BATTLE TO THE DEATH ... 22-41

INTERLUDE THREE 44-45

THE HUNTING GROUNDS 46-63

THE ENDLESS STAIRCASE 64-75

INTERLUDE ONE

ANOTHER DRINK, another slingshot into oblivion—the man slumped heavily against the counter in a small modular home on a hill above a bottomless pit, where liquid methane flowed like magma whenever tidal forces warmed the icy moon of Titan.

The man blacked out and collapsed onto the floor as the effects of the drink hit his system violently. His last rational image was of a blurry spiral of fleeting objects ranging from the replicator bar to the carpet as he hit the ground.

He choked on the cocktail of scotch gas and chickpea pretzel bites that erupted from his stomach as the spilled vapor drifted about the room lazily like a drunken ghost.

FROM THE LUMINOUS bands of the Milky Way, a speck warps into a white hole vortex. Out of the portal bursts a particle—smaller than a tau, but with a tail trillion of light years long—rolling on a dark energy lightning bolt powered by a black hole engine.

The particle's journey ends at the feet of the man who collapsed on the floor, and its construct begins to dissipate, revealing a temporal being who does not exist in any past, present, or future incarnation of this universe. The rider stands before the body, and with some irritation, he kicks the corpse awake from its eternal nap.

"You'd like to sleep off this existence, wouldn't you? Just slide off into death again and again. But you have visions to behold and wisdom to gain this time."

The man was confused and neglected to respond. He did not want to participate actively during this stupor and wondered why a trespasser in synthetic chaps, sporting many mismatching tentacle eyes, was bothering him.

"You will listen and learn. What you see will not be repeated," spoke the being clearly and purposefully. "You have a one-way ticket where you're going."

The man's only reaction was to try to change out of his vomit-soaked clothes clumsily as he stared at the trespasser with a terrible maw and wandering eyes. He failed miserably to dress as his legs transformed into bands of separating matter that spread to the rest of his body, morphing him entirely into a hovering ball with a wavering aura and colorful hues.

The man was hysterical as the room shifted from beige fittings and bay windows to a swirl of black and sharp pinpoints of white. Words failed to express his whirling thoughts as his frantic ego sought the vocabulary to describe his conscious state to his clamoring id. He wished for something logical to emerge, some reasonable image to take shape on his inner chalkboard. Something, anything to anchor his ego, which was presently adrift on the current of infinite shades of existence during its transformation into the organic form of an atman, filtered through the kaleidoscope of multistability.

His visage was a million-degree view of unlimited possibilities flitting in between realities, stacked in rainbow layers until the fractal structure of the universe congealed into a display of silvery spheres floating between wormholes.

His only sensation was the tug on his form as it began to spaghettify and spool into the twisting morass of energy that is the machine. The pair are instantly transported to the near future and spit out before the Sun.

INTERLUDE ONE

THE STAR FARMER

THE SUN DOMINATED the landscape, providing A steady yield of light with no regard to any notion of dawn or dusk. The Earth, hungry for power, paid a premium for it, while only the middle man made the coin, and the gatherer got the short end of the stick.

Still, the Farmer stood tall while perusing Mercury's horizon; out before him, a vista filled with fields of silicon carbon panels floating on magnetic buffers in perfect, harmonious symmetry. His farm covered hundreds of arc miles rich in territorial bounty, and his boards hauled higher yields than any other farm. Nevertheless, he sought the big haul that had eluded his family for generations.

The Farmer toiled in his fields, clearing away the little pebbles that landed on the solar panels—the inconvenient aftermath of the latest stellar storm. His automated sweepers did a fine job of removing the dust, but with rocks, the objects scratched the surface of the panels, reducing their efficiency and collection capabilities. In short order, the Farmer managed to clean the collectors and keep his schedule on track.

His family had worked the land for generations, and he was the latest Farmer to keep their almanac current. The worn book gave him an edge against the other farmers who had only recently arrived and could not fully utilize the Sun's varying flow. His family recorded the quirks of the increasingly erratic star. The almanac predicted a large harvest—the Titan, an anomaly foreseen to cause an enormous solar storm.

The other farmers feared the coming storm, but he remained undaunted. The ambitious Farmer was ready to face the dangers of this excellent yield. His experience extended past typical arrays to snagging solar flares in eruption. He monitored the brewing storm and deduced which face would erupt and spill forth the intense plasma stream, and he applied the appropriate countermeasures to his collection units.

Since Mercury's north pole harbored transformers hardwired to the planet's liquid iron core, suspended in acid imported from Venus, the other planets faced a lessened chance of a fiery death. Mercury was the perfect storage unit for the harvested solar power because its easily manipulated weak magnetic field aided in channeling the Sun's output. On the planet's surface, the collection units rested on magnetic buffers in beds of bunkers; their task was to absorb the flare blast, which required a seamless skin to maximize collection and maintain structural integrity during overloading energy spikes.

The Farmer charged against the clock to work out the bugs while the computers worked through the automated linking program. Just as important as the upcoming harvest was the special occasion that day—a day of significance that he would never forget.

It was the 222nd day of the year and celebrated as the day Pa met Ma, and the day they tied the knot. He had to make it home to the orbiting station on the planet's dark side in time for dinner. He worked quickly, never missing an anniversary with his wife. He also had never missed a birthday celebration for his three kids, who had all been purposefully born on day 314 to make things more convenient. Ma's birthday, however, was on day 42, which had always been disappointing for her, for it lined up with the solar celebration, and she had always been overshadowed and shorted on that day since childhood. His wife paged him as he entered the command dome in his dusty boots.

"Pa! Ya got visitors coming—some government folks. Don't know why," sputtered Ma in a fuzzy chain of static and words. The calls between the dark side of the planet and the farm were always a garbled, disrupted affair.

"Who?"

"The government! Said you gotta stay out of their way," replied Ma.

"All righty then! It looks like I need to get cleaned up. I'm hungry. I won't be late, Ma," offered Pa with a smile as he motioned one-four-three with his fingers and then cut off the feed. The sign language helped compensate for the blipping signal during conversations.

Pa headed to the showers to make himself presentable. Afterward, he swept the bay of the dirt from his earlier entry and set about wrapping up the day's business by performing a remote panel assessment to determine if he could finally head home. The line was active again.

"Hello, Government," said Pa to the man on the screen.

"Are you Pa, as your lovely wife spoke of?" asked a female voice from somewhere off-screen.

"Yep! What is this about? Our lease is legal," replied the Farmer.

"Open the shields to the pad and extend the dome. We need to come in," snapped the man bluntly.

"Okay," said Pa as he turned the switch.

The government ship landed in the marked zone as the shields closed. The gangway of the dome extended to the shuttle. The Earthlings exited their ship and soon entered the farm's command center.

"Welcome," declared Pa hospitably.

"This is a federal matter. We need your assistance immediately. And by 'assistance,' we mean that we need to seize your base for an undetermined duration, and you need to go home," demanded the lead scientist without a shred of courtesy.

"Um, ya gotta explain… You gots no eminent domain on the Mercury," urged the Farmer.

"These guns and your sense of decency," barked the lead scientist while gesturing toward his soldiers. He didn't seem very interested in discussing civil rights.

"Sorry for the rush, but the Sun is about to sneeze!" interrupted a younger female scientist standing nearby. She was presumably his assistant.

"Yep! Tis be my payday. Got a yield to snare, so please just let me be. Feel free to refresh yourselves or use the facilities. Just don't mess with meh settings," compromised the Farmer. "Typical Earthers," he added under his breath.

The scientist ignored the Farmer as he directed the inflow of boxes and equipment carried from his ship.

"Based on what we know about solar dynamics, there shouldn't be any mystery as to why the Sun may wreak havoc on her children," said the assistant scientist.

The yellow star was a mellow, stable mother with bipolar disorder. Her magnetic field flipped, and another violent whiplash was sure to hit, violating her previous predictable twelve-year cycle of calm magnetic variance. The scientists dug into their records, seeking any explanation for the Sun's schizophrenic behavior.

The Farmer returned to the group and spoke without invitation, "I reckon, in my records, I gotcha answer. My family recorded the yields, and—"

"Guards, do your job and pull this hick back." The lead scientist's sour face wrinkled even further as he gave the Farmer a look.

"Just give it a perusal at your convenience," offered the Farmer as he placed the almanac down for them to look at on their own.

He reviewed the status of his array on the display panel one last time and headed out before the guards could touch him. He smiled on his way out of the base, for his array was in perfect order based on the variance he'd predicted. He was eager to leave the rude government agents behind, and his delicious anniversary dinner awaited him.

The hungry Farmer mumbled as he jumped into his tractor, "Settled 'Mury' ages ago. We were the first settlers on this frontier. Those rocket babies should check my records. The Titan's the answer." The Farmer managed to cover about half the distance between the base and home when his frustrated rambling was cut short by a call on his radio.

"Pa," asked the woman scientist, "are you there? We made a mistake and accidentally moved one of your panels."

"Golly, now I gotta get to fixing my fields," groaned the Farmer. "T'was almost home. I gots to tell you that we've seen this storm before. You guys don't pay any attention. You all focused on the outer planets and stuff. My grandpappy used to talk about the egg-shaped spheres that live in the Sun and their influence of the mag cycles… the Titan storms."

"How long do we have to listen to his hick jabber on about conspiracy theories?" spat the lead scientist impatiently.

"Have some respect for the locals," defended the assistant. "There is some validity to his supposition."

"Not gonna give me their ear," grumbled the Farmer as he continued his duty. "Messing with my equipment. I might do something about it but ain't got the time. Too hungry for meh vittles." The Farmer shrugged off his irritation and growling stomach as he drove. He had to restart his routine to find and sort out the problem the Earthlings had caused, and he had to do it in haste before the storm hit, or else he'd lose the bounty.

The Farmer's tractor hovered above the array range. He quickly spotted the two sections that had rammed together. He knew the panels had to be raised to the proper angle and height to capture and endure the blast. Otherwise, the integrity of the structure would collapse.

Back at the dome, the lead scientist bantered about the Farmer's homespun superstitious lore, ignoring the book the Farmer had left behind as he barked orders to his crew. "The seismometers report a 150% increase of radiobanit waves, tachyon particles to follow. The first sign that the flare is—"

"I got my equipment in the dome. I need some help, ya governmentals," requested Pa. He remotely overrode the schematics present on his master view screen, cutting off the speaker in the command center. "You'll just need to press the green and red buttons for me."

"Do what the sunburn needs," replied the lead scientist.

His aide clicked the buttons, and the solar arrays in those fields moved into position.

"The spot check is complete—quite the haul. I should call Ma. Let her know about my delay." The Farmer tried to dial his wife, but the increased magnetic activity from the Sun interfered with the reception. He was supposed to be under the dome or on the dark side during a storm—never in the open.

The Farmer burned more fuel and oxygen on his return to the safety of his base, now filled with the bustle of locals in a panic due to the Government's arrival. He buzzed the door to gain entry to his dome. No one answered, and he wondered why they locked him out of his facility. The Farmer returned to his tractor. He attempted to radio Ma again, but the signal was dead. On the sensor bank, an indicator blinked yellow, then red.

"Gosh darn it! The far-field in the green sector is out of place again. Meh, dinner's going to get cold."

A tinny squawk blasted the dome's radio, "The Sun is losing mass, the hydrogen levels are clipping and in reduction. Helium levels increasing. Indicators show a fiery belch is brewing. She's going flare any time," the panicked scientist broadcast his message across the entire planet, further panicking the residents.

The Farmer fired up his tractor. He had work to do. He headed back to the fields for the green sector. It was a ten-minute drive, and time was running out. Over a given week, he'd have to replace a panel or two in his fields. Today was not the day for that statistic to inconvenience him for any kink in the array during the storm would trigger a catastrophic plasma wave that would smother Mercury's face.

The tractor limped over the ridge and down to the gully that spilled into the field where the panels rested. The Sun filled the horizon, and the Farmer would be blind to the incoming flare when it hit.

The damaged section was on the far edge, opposite from his approach. The Farmer continued on his route, straight above the protective panels, to cut down the distance, though it increased his chances of a fiery death during his fly-by survey. The trip was slow. The Farmer's palms were sweaty. He nervously passed over the two cracked panels and one that a fist-sized meteorite had utterly smashed. The star's magnetic disturbances had sent several iron chunks of space rocks hurtling wayward into his boards. Their replacement panels lay in storage sheds conveniently located close to the array. The trip would be short, as would be the repair time for the two cracked panels.

First, he had to get the scientists to move his array, but they did not answer his ping. The Farmer desperately buzzed them again for assistance. Still no answer. He would have to replace the panel manually. It was a tricky affair as the Farmer entered the empty metal frame and manually removed the stuck, jagged shards of silicon carbon.

It was a dangerous job. The space suit caught on several sharp slivers during the task, ripping several small holes into the fabric. The Farmer stopped to repair it and continued preparing the 25 by 20-foot sections. Time was running out, and every second counted. He used the last repair tape on the tears in his suit and then tried to contact the dome to close out the procedure. Unsurprisingly, the call was unsuccessful due to the increased solar activity. He was still on his own. He had two more tasks; his oxygen was running dangerously low, and the taped holes still leaked precious air.

Finally cleared of debris, the Farmer hopped back to the shed to retrieve the new panel. The storm should have already hit, but fortunately, the Sun had delayed its blazing gift.

He knew that the face of the storm had changed, the blast strength determined by the position of the space egg plaguing the Sun. He was in place for the first storm face and knew that the others followed in a reasonably predictable wave; still, the fine adjustments had to be made based on the information in his book. However, since he had left the almanac with the scientists, he would have to make do with what he could remember, for communication with the dome was impossible.

The Farmer set about his final repair, knowing that while the Earth had an eight-minute buffer, his time was scant in comparison. He had about 120 seconds from the eruption to when the crest kissed his panels, but he had even less time to escape the storm safely. He would have only mere seconds from the solar eruption, for what preceded the crest was just as dangerous as the flare itself, and with no shielding atmosphere, he was on the front line—wholly exposed.

The tractor was low on fuel at takeoff. The Sun's gravity held tight to the craft, trying to gently pull it away from Mercury's grasp during the slow trek. The new panel dragged behind the tractor, parallel to the array. It was time, and the Farmer unlatched his cargo. The board floated below the tractor and began to drift away. He set the controls for the tractor to crash land at the end of the fields, safely away from the collection units, to avoid damaging them.

The Farmer slid down from the cabin to the fuel tank and leaped toward the panel. The short jump ended when he took control by planting his feet to surf the board. It was a smooth, gentle glide down to his beloved array—his first moment of peace this afternoon. He took a few seconds of the bulging Sun during his descent, his aching eyes barely protected by the visor. He tilted the panel left, then right as he corrected course and neared his final objective half blind. He was confident the plan would fail.

Despite his reservations, the Farmer landed on the array with a limp slap on the collectors' surface, breaking his

numerous rules about using scratched units. He slid the last scale missing in the link without wasting time and set it to adjust the array for the next face. With his skilled hands, the collection unit was in order within seconds. He'd done it. Mercury was saved.

The sensor pulsed and squeezed his arm, signaling the start of the storm. He could not reach his tractor in time to drive somewhere safe to escape the blast. The Farmer turned to face the flare as it raged forward.

"Ninety seconds or so, I reckon. Damn, the radio is out. I gots the arc coordinator numerator though. Ma's gonna to kill me if I don't send word." The dismayed Farmer had an idea.

He furiously keyed **00001432220423140000** into arc coordinator numerator before the flare hit him. His form transformed into plasma absorbed by the panels of his beloved fields.

INTERLUDE TWO

THE RIDER spurred the man forward in chase after the farmer's soul— into the machine, to tumble about the pins of possibilities, into holes of chance that wait all along the continuum.

Gravity took its toll on the man's form with each entry and exit. He witnessed streams of light, which at first had passed them and which they would later pass. He sensed that the journey was instantaneous yet infinite, as static electricity sparked their advancement by flipping their polarities to speeds faster than light.

The two beings are spat out of the machine a million years into the future before a misshapen moon long consigned to its fate.

"Where are we now?" asked the man upon exit.

"A semiotic pit stop along the crossroads of Déjà Vu. The best junction points for travel are often when the machine opens to swallow a soul freed from its chora."

"So, you're not a god," stated the man flatly. "You're just some creep lurking in the shadows, hitching rides."

"I exist like you do. As to 'gods,' I've never met one, but I'll keep an eye peeled."

BATTLE TO THE DEATH

THE GALACTIC CONGRESS of space-faring species ruled again on a case where the troublesome hominids and robots had caused another headache for the fading star park known as the Milky Way.

The Congress pursued a solution that would rid them of the vermin that brought uncertainty to their existence. To end the human's drag race through civilized space in pursuit of a new home ever since the extinction of their yellow star when the Ontario eggs hatched inside it. Similarly, the Galactic Congress had grown weary of the planet-sized collector robots filling storage tanks with sentient hydrogen atoms while feigning ignorance that these ethereal forms harbored intelligent life.

The Empire's solution took shape when an errant space probe inadvertently unleashed a catastrophic energy flare as it aimlessly explored a set of planets on a long-forgotten cataloging mission—sent on its expedition ages ago from a now abandoned Earth. The robots' ecosystem was a star-spanning power sphere that provided a constant source of freely flowing energy in the space that filled their verse.

The probe inadvertently triggered the one weakness of the system as a tidal feedback loop led to a terrible robopocalypse started by the ungrounded unit. The robot survivors seized the interloper and determined its source—their age-old rivals—the humans. The paranoid robots thought they had been attacked and set about petitioning the Galactic Government. The humans were first bemused by the robots' accusations and then shocked by the court's citation for 'littering,' ultimately making them culpable for the disaster. The humans demanded an appeal and refused to accept the blame, while the outraged robots demanded retribution. Sadly, the two sides had to fight to the death by order of the Galactic Congress.

A hundred years later, the last human supply ship warped into the system adjacent to their final destination, a vaguely familiar dilapidated planet orbiting a splintered star. To make the long trip, they transitioned into genetic information to be respawned in specialized growth chambers on arrival. Unknowingly, they now faced the last days of humanity.

TOWERING MECHANICAL BEASTS of varied assemblage roamed the battlefield, filling the soundscape with the grind of massive gears and the hollow cadence of gigantic metal feet pounding the rocky ground, step after each clanging step. The Titan-wielding Combots swept the carnage of past engagements from their path by flinging the husks of damaged tanks into the air with their strong clamps. Rusty reconnaissance probes blended in the sooty plumes of smoke staining the amber skyline as they chased after their objective, an incoming human supply ship, calculating if its imminent landing site was available for retrieval by the scavenger bots.

The cyborg squad followed the metal giants, stealthily out of sight and out of reach of the robots' wide, crushing swings, which could easily tear their human flesh and bone. Meanwhile, floating sentience-seeking sensor bombs sought to stir the mammals from their hiding spaces with small, tactical nuclear strikes. Hovering gun batteries scanned the heavens for the supplies and reinforcements the humans desperately needed, which their mechanical enemy planned to scavenge for their resources.

"Go, go, go!" ordered the First Sergeant to her company.

The squad leaders understood the orders. They sought to storm the complex containing the factory that manufactured Titans sourced from battlefield remains. The Titans were substantial mechanical battle armor suits that the Combots piloted against the humans in the war; the humans needed to take some of the suits as their own to have any fighting chance against their robotic foes.

The ragtag team executed the orders without question. Their comrades distracted the enemy outside while they secured the unguarded robots within.

The company entered the factory floor from the sloped entryway. The air was thick and heavy with fumes, but the room was rich and heavy with spoils.

The strike team secured fifteen fresh Titans lined up neatly in an underground storage bay under the planet's surface. The cyborgs split up, and each picked a beast to reengineer. They had only seconds to commandeer the massive robots before the security sensors triggered automatic destruction sequences for the unimprinted giants.

The First Sergeant scanned her pad to track the progress of the strike. She uncomfortably shifted her weight between the metal and human half of her body. The fittings of her augmentations were not precise, so she always had to shuffle her weight to compensate for her legs of varying height and the importance of the guns built into her left arm.

Ironically, both sides had, over time, assumed characteristics of their enemy over the hundred-year tour. The first Combot was a versions apart from those leading the battle today. Their corecode was altered by honing their counter-logic response tactics against the unpredictable mammals over the years, thus making their thought processes more human than robot. Conversely, humans became more metal than damaged and sported mechanical parts.

The human cyborgs also constantly feared being infected by malicious code coursing in the leftover hardware sourced from robot debris. Their worst fears were that the Combots could embed a dormant senescence countermeasure within some of the Titans' servos, waiting to initiate a packet of directives triggered when infected cyborgs would man errant robots. Susceptible cyborgs would discover their infection too late, as the code began the self-destruct module in the Titan.

Despite the danger, the brave human cyborgs still placed themselves in the robot skins. They jacked into the Titan by inserting their connector prods, providing the necessary command ports to run the robot's various sections. The entire operation was analogous to a dinosaur requiring many tiny brains to strut its massive girth.

The metallic mechs were juiced, and the focused hackers calibrated the operation of the beasts. Meanwhile, the robots on the wild human chase outside had caught on to the diversion once the base's emergency signals finally went off in a flashing blare of sirens.

In response, the humans shelled the incoming force with well-aimed EMP mortars. The Titans would take hours to reboot from the circuit fry as redundant backup systems replaced the damaged units. The gods of war were smiling on the human side, for the enemy's dreaded gun platforms were too far out of range to reach the factory before the humans escaped.

The team had to move on, or the angry Combots would catch up. Luckily, the robots searching for the other humans were still too engaged in the heated chase to return for the missing Titans. The one immediate response to the humans' presence was the appearance of the repair bots in the vicinity. They buzzed furiously against the stolen Titans, attempting to gain entry in the robot suits and stop the human intruders.

This mission had been in the planning stages since they had received word of the incoming supply ship—thought lost to the stars decades ago—and a few rust buckets wouldn't get in their way.

"T14 under attack," reported the squad leader, riding in the cramped control deck of the Titan's head. "Buzz bots overran the mid-section, still running. Drawing power off extremities."

The humans covered their general bases by sealing off the direct entries into the mechs. Still, the flying repair bots knew the Titans' blueprints and could quickly engineer an alternate entrance. The most common intrusion point would be through the knee or elbow joints, where thin metal mesh covers the articulations to keep sand and rocks out of the gears. The repair bots possessed cutting shears that could easily slice through this mesh and gain entry, but fortunately, their options to reach a programming station inside were very limited from thc extremities.

The First Sergeant chimed in, "Ignore the pests! We have a distance to cover to get to the crossroads and then a detour through the rocky valley. We bypass the bridging crag. T13, bear off, and pull back! You have the rear point."

"Aye, Firstie," replied T13.

"T3 through T12, keep a separation of two clicks… and secure the airspace above sector ten," she added.

The humans knew once the Combots detected their procession, they would descend on the leading group and complicate plans. The prevailing idea was that the robots would mass at the crag; it was the only viable crossing for the Titans and the best location to take potshots at the incoming supply ship heading for the human quadrant. The Combots had received the same message the humans did and planned to act on the intelligence.

"Firstie! T14 in flight. We left the package."

The First Sergeant witnessed the evidence of the statement as the core blew, and the glare of a nuclear flare visible from kilometers away broadcast their former location to the robots.

"T14, shadow the squad!" shouted the First Sergeant.

The line of hijacked Titans marched before the setting amber star, whose dying light glinted across their battered armor weakly as they hit the crossroads. The sergeant ordered her comrades T3 through T14 to the rocky valley while T2 stayed behind to set up a distraction to ensure the other Titans reached the rendezvous point. They had to walk out on the flattened paths nestled between muddy fields choked with decades of ghastly, gnarled robot remains and abandoned battle tanks filled with unlucky human crews in boggy graves. The going was treacherous by foot, as they had to pass over sinkholes and trenches or through giant coils of barbed wire.

T14 served as the group's eyes and hovered over the Titans. Time passed slowly while the First Sergeant received the squad's progress. The Combots' surveillance probes had already located the hijacked Titans.

"Sarge! The analysis determined the entire region is unsteady because of decades of mining. Seeking route," reported T6.

A pack of twenty enemy Combots in Titans and a swarm of scavenger bots descended after them on the crossroads—the clogged northern path filled up with incoming heavy metal. Fortunately, the eastern course was empty, and the west was free due to an earlier nuclear blast that delivered its fiery tidings to their metal foes.

T2 laid a trap with a clutch of reprogrammed droids, filling the path. The droids' orders were to apply suppressive fire while under his control as he conducted a violent chorus with motions that the little droid army would mirror. "T2 reporting. In position."

"T2, fire at your discretion," relayed the sergeant.

The incoming scavbots—the unarmed garbage bots of the field—posed no threat, but in great numbers, they could dissemble an isolated Titan in quick order, like how an army of ants could chase down and pick apart a wounded animal. The scavbots failed to approach the crossroads before being cut down by the droids, whose power cells were draining quickly. Soon, the droid's batteries would drain dry.

"T2 still holding. Droids killed the majority of thc first swarm. The Titans are closing in. Preparing mortars."

T2 remained in a position to influence control of the droids, as the operational range was a very limiting distance of less than a mile. They would engage the new wave of tenacious scavbots returning for more abuse. It looked like the engagement would be an casy win.

"T2 reporting. Road clogged with dead scavbots. The Titans are in flight over the field, avoiding the path. The 'bots have learned to avoid combat with lone robots," he stated smugly.

"T2, pull the plug and join us in the crags," barked the sergeant.

He complied and set the droids to "proximity mine" mode, programmed to explode on approach by any large object. "T2 reporting. Laid the eggs! Leaving crossroads mined. Will mirror Titans crossing the range."

The squad was still in pursuit of a solution, and the enemy Titans quickly marching across the range counter to their position changed the humans' strategy from a steady retreat to a deadly game of hide-and-seek.

"Status," ordered the sergeant.

"T6 tracking path. The only solution is to climb the cliffs, looking for an entry point. Promising flat ahead. No enemy detected."

"CO reporting. Top, the supply ship's arrival is on target," interjected the commander from the human quadrant.

"Aye, Sir," replied the First Sergeant, "Rodger that. Over and out." She glanced at her squad and gestured. "Make some stairs! We will be coming in hot and heavy. T2, follow T14's lead!"

"T6 reporting... Blasted the walls! A hundred meters high, ascension possible. Sending coordinates."

"T2 reporting, Titans have split off a dozen of the twenty. What should we do, Top?"

"Do not engage. Mirror and retreat! Work to join us at the crags," the sergeant replied. She wanted to avoid any unnecessary firefighting and bloodshed.

"Aye. Understood."

"T6 reporting. Scaled stairs, ten clicks east to the edge. Horizon scan reveals no blips, Sarge."

"Head to the edge. Hold position," she responded.

"T6 reporting. The path is clear. I reached the halfway point. Horizon scan clear."

"T14 reporting. Titans have reached the entrance of the valley. Ten in pursuit of our pack."

"Maintain trajectory."

"T6 reporting. Reached the edge! Horizon scan reveals no enemy."

"Hold position, T6," ordered the sergeant, planning their moves. "T2, use your fuel to jump the cliffs."

"T14 reporting. Holding at midpoint. Titans between us and the edge."

"T3 through T12, you will lay down suppressive fire while retreating to the edge, but on my order," directed the sergeant. "Hold your fire, or else you betray our position." The long train of giant robots needed to reach the edge of the cliffs but not become a target in the process.

"Aye!" replied the squad leaders.

"T14 reporting. Horizon scan reveals a mining tank. Tracking."

"T2!" the First Sergeant barked. "Track south away from us, and then backtrack to the edge once the enemy moves away from us." She knew the risk of sending him out as a decoy again but couldn't let the Combots bring their tank any closer.

The Combots were confused by the voluntary splintering of the human party, as their programming deemed the continuing fracturing of their forces illogical. The cannon they drove had a minimal range and posed little threat to the human quadrant. The robot command worked to devise a priority list to nail with the tank's plasma gun, which they began to use with painfully good aim.

"T9 reporting. Under fire! T4 and T5 nailed and down. No recovery effort, full man down."

"Regrets T9, continue on route. You are in range until the edge. Our position is still in hiding."

"T9 copy."

The robot command did not take long to ascertain that the scattered scouts were heading for the main party, which was still hiding. First Sergeant, realizing this, ordered their large guns to fire before their departure and before the Combots could act on the main party. They would give the robots their position but cheat them of their victory.

"Fire on the cannon," she ordered.

A volley of fireballs exited the squad's cannons and blasted towards the Combots' position. Five shots nailed their tank cannon's platform and turned off the massive crawler, thus rendering it immobile. The enemy Titans dodged in time and remained unscathed. They hurried towards the source of the mortar fire.

"T2 reporting... drawing fire." He was under attack by the enemy. His Titan shell's right leg had been struck by a Combot's fireball, severely slowing the pace at which he could retreat up the cliffs.

"T2, abandon your craft and transport to T7. Set the Titan to 'proximity mine' status. The robots' scan will reveal it, and they will avoid our position while we jump."

T2 took a direct hit to the head of the Titan before the cyborg inside could respond to the First Sergeant's order. The fiery blast melted the frame of the metal giant and the man inside with a bath of scorching fire. The fiery craft was now molten lead, crashing fast to the rocky moon's surface.

"T2, report!" ordered the First Sergeant. She feared the worst had happened—yet another comrade lost! There was no time to reflect. She viewed the vast landscape before her that was the moon's core. They must make the thousand-kilometer leap to the human quadrant to escape.

The Titans jetted off the edge, one after another until the entire squad had jumped into the gulf. They floated across the gaping divide that was once the barren body of a moon, now two halves separated by a massive rocky crag.

They crossed the span altogether. Occasional slight jetting blasts pushed the group forward to the human quadrant during their two-day airborne journey. The robots failed to follow them and were confident that the humans had disappeared into the void.

THE NEW RECRUITS had arrived. their emergence from biotube to operational status driven by Autobots that guided the process. Two sliding doors opened to reveal a large bay.

"Shake it off and grab your gear," cooed a synthetic female voice over the intercom, programmed with some sass. It was just what the troops needed to hear while waking up and vomiting the bitter retransformation fluid from their guts.

Gus, a first-year recruit in the infantry, watched the others as he pulled on his gear. Easy to slide on, it was a one-piece habitation suit, and he only had to climb in and zip up. Over time, the battle suit would modify its form as it conformed to the body shape of its wearer and hydrated the emaciated trooper. For now, though, it was an uncomfortable, bulky outfit and heavy in the ship's artificial gravity.

"Proceed to the main hangar bay and fall into formation," continued the artificial voice.

The proceedings were dour and without ceremony. No music. No flags. Only the sound of the computer's voice greeted the troops. The fresh meat group gathered in the bay and assembled before the First Sergeant, holding court in the center.

"Welcome to Battle Moon. Our field of combat is where we are to resolve our century-long conflict with the rust buckets with extreme violence. As you briefed, your term of service on this moon is until victory or death."

She clicked a button on an electronic band she sported on her left arm. Large doors opened to a bay with soldiers seated behind metal tables. First Sergeant, or Top, as some called her, was a tall woman with scars from cheek to chin, coldly framed with quietly whirring mechanical limbs. The woman was hard and seasoned, giving the troops confidence that survival was possible.

"Normally, we would just toss you into the grinder and let the fates sort you out, but there has been a twist. While A.W.O.L in space, the war has raged for nearly a century. Much faster ships, including some folks here today, took your place in the conflict." She looked around the room meaningfully, making eye contact with her squad members as she continued. "We knew about your ship and fought generations knowing you'd arrive some day.

"The veterans, myself included, have been haunted by the fears of your supply ship bleeping into robot airspace, and you don't want to know the horrors that await any humans in their clutch. You are the last fertile children of Earth. You are released from the burden of combat and will now return to the Alpha Centari ring city where you'd find yourself welcome. The final battle is coming."

The bay was buzzing with confused and surprised mumbles by the newly awoken reinforcements. The First Sergeant approached Gus, who could not find a table. She had kind eyes on her hardened face and softened her features as the young man stared at her silently, in a daze. She pulled him aside from the crowd and spoke to him.

"I have so much to say, but I will be brief. I am your daughter Anna, and for decades, I have fought. After learning about your ship's fate, I fought even harder. Mom told me so much about you. I wish I could spend more time with you, but we are mounting an offensive that end this war, and time is of the essence."

She smiled warmly and offered her oversized metal hand in search of a shake. Gus stiffened and shook back. His twenty-nine-year-old hands were still weak from the long hibernation, and he was in shock from finding out that he had a daughter, especially one who was now even older than he was. She saluted, then turned, ending the awkward exchange.

"We live on!," announced the First Sergeant to her troops, "to victory!

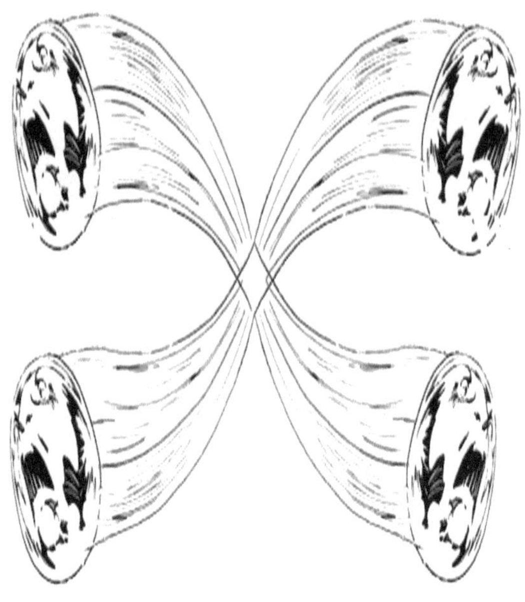

INTERLUDE THREE

THE RIDER ONCE again spurred the man on into the machine—other spheres headed in separate directions about their infinite paths. The being ended their drag race against tachyons and photons, and the exit produced the same brown dwarf, except a ring of rocky skin now surrounded it. A giant rock dominated its smaller neighbors with the pull of gravity from its mass.

"Who are you?" asked the man finally.

"Isn't that the question you should ask yourself?" retorted the being cryptically. "What does it matter who I am? Still, I am no different from you, but I am someone who unties quantum knots and herds rocats. I mainly sweep loose infinities into the great dust bin."

"So, you're the universal custodian," jested the man.

"Ha, you can say that. The universe is a layered matrix, perfect in existence. It is unexplainable, ever-changing, and if reality skips, I clean the smear."

"Am I the smear?" asked the man.

"Enough! Without the appropriate experience, you have no context, no meaning. Your vocabulary will fail to describe your position. Try to see and not speak. Start by focusing on the pulsating machine. Look to the edges of the hole. Look beyond the reification your sense of self creates to shape the unknown. You have not seen this before and are not even seeing it now, for it is merely a symbolic construction you've rationalized. You must break the barrier of rational thought and focus on presence, not awareness. You are blind, yet you see. You have already sensed that you have no eyes, ears, or limbs, no sense of boundary or edge, yet you have a sense of self and ambition. The real lesson is to learn how to put a harness on your thoughts."

The man was silent. He reflected along with the being as time ticked by in million-year clips. He wondered about the bull crap his kidnapper was feeding him as the panoramic view before the pair changed and evolved. Entropy furiously beat their surroundings with a stick, and the lulling passage of time enabled the man to care not if the being's speeches were spouts of universal truth and he held his tongue.

THE HUNTING GROUNDS

EONS PAST, the last stars were murdered by the tug of invisible giants who forced the gas bodies to collapse in supernova fury and stage a final glorious solar charge; the quasars slowly slurped and savored the stars' last gasp of hope, and ultimately, they ended the era of stars. The universe was beginning to show its age, scarred by black hole rainbows rolling throughout dimensions like wheels on a Brahman tricycle—a colorful funeral procession for life that still had about another billion-year run, living by the residual glow in a rapidly expanding universe.

THE ONTARO migrated in successive waves, back to the ancient spawning grounds, from the mating nebula on the other side of the dead Milky Way galaxy. A vast expanse of perilous hazards and dangerous gravity swells haunted the present space. The last Ontaro pod made the big push for the nursery on the tail end of a two-hundred-million-year circuit.

At that time, the Kaku had moved in to fill the void of sentience in the region. The Kaku, the last children of space, did not have lungs; instead, they absorbed ambient energy and microscopic particles through their conductive skin suits. However, they required more energy and nutrition than the skin could passively collect around the dead star, so the arrival of the Ontaro heralded a new age for the Kaku—the metal men.

They benefitted from the Ontaro pods' ignorance, as the beasts had followed their instinctively hardwired space coordinates to this gauntlet of icy rocks for millions of years to rest, feed, and spawn. They were weary, gravid, and easy to kill at this point in their migration.

The Kaku had long forgotten about life outside their rocks and lived for the hunt. Great honor and tribal prizes awaited the hunters with the best haul. They never even let one Ontaro reach the failed star, demonstrating their prowess as a hunting tribe.

The kills were put to good use, as the Kaku would use the rich Ontaro eggs as highly nutritious food stores and could even make them into crude explosives. The tough pelts could be traded or tanned for making suits. All carcasses were valued, as they were the primary source of tools used in hunting. Shell and bone became hooks, knives, and harpoons. Sinew fibers braided into ropes or nets for hunting. They sourced everything they could for any purpose they required.

Arto, the big male bull, led this Ontaro pod. They circled the nursery, seeking entry, still unaware of the hunters or the trying gauntlet they would have to run. Arto relished the thought of the comforting pressures of the star and the songs that the future hatchlings would sing. His group had only five females in it—the smallest of the recent wave of Ontaro.

The metalmen spotted their pod and passed hand signals between the hunters. The Kaku had no means of traveling across the asteroid belt other than daring leaps between the rocks, using their skin capes as sails, or using twisted sinew ropes to guide their journey between their caves and the rocky belt that served as the hunting grounds.

The hunters took their spots on various rocks to hide and await their prey. Once the bull decided the route and led his pod through the belt, the hunters would act, firing their torpedo harpoons. If they landed a successful hit, the struck Ontaro would try to escape, slowly dragging the firmly an-

chored rock of the harpooner. Other hunters would cast nets to immobilize their prey for the kill.

One mistimed hit could sour the hunt and divert the group of frightened Ontaro back into the black of space. The hunters employed a wide range of methods to try to prevent this. Some of the tribe stood on the fertile hunting grounds while others occupied outlying spots that required guile and the luck that the wounded Ontaro passed their position.

Chuk, the lead hunter of the Zut clan, held the stone furthest from the home rock. They would take on the slow or wounded if the bull did not change their position. The hunters of his clan were in their usual places to cover the approach of any prey that circled the brown dwarf before taking the plunge in. He looked forward to bringing fat, egg-laden females home for a great feast. His clan was skilled at breaking down the beasts efficiently. They even assisted other tribes, often with disassembling their bounty.

Arto spied the large rock but failed to notice the stealthy hunters leaping from stone to stone. After making four wide circles, the bull realized there was no easy route to their intended nursery. Frustrated, Arto began to lead the females into a thicket of rocks of lesser density in the thick asteroid belt surrounding the brown dwarf.

Without notice, the male was met with hit after hit as harpoons pierced and exploded in the hard skin of the bull. Several of the spears were hooked painfully into his flesh. The explosive tips breaking off outer shell pieces forced the creature to expose its tender underbelly. The fleeing bull dragged along the hunters' asteroid stations as the harpoon was anchored to the rocks by strong sinew ropes. The brave hunters were honored with the opportunity to crawl across the rope and finish the kill. Many men scrambled along the rocks and sought to pierce the tough hide with the sharpened rib bones of Ontaro, past slain, resurrected as daggers and spears designed to kill their brethren.

The rocks, strung to the harpoons piercing the male's skin, whipped about as he fiercely twisted in an attempt to wrest himself free, pulling the hunters into a spiral around him. The ambushed male was weak from the long journey and soon succumbed in his struggle against the hunters, who were now working on pulling the body into the orbit of their home rock.

The frightened females scattered from the dangerous path where Arto suffered damage. The tribes realigned their hunting team, and those on the flanks converged on two young females veering up into a tangle of nets. Another Ontaro was hooked near the edge of the asteroid belt, having almost reached the safety of open space. Like him, the senior female was not much luckier than the bull and was taken down brutally by numerous harpoons and spears. Many hunters were left wondering about the dozens more females expected to follow, not realizing that this small batch was the last of them.

Huna, the last of the Ontaro, changed her course once she caught sight of the hunters slaughtering her pod. Based on past encounters, she knew enough to hide when danger appeared and to emerge only when the male's call assured safety. Except this time, she saw the bull slain and the alpha female stabbed. They were most certainly dead. Her heart ached for her two doomed sisters, and this massacre only added to her deep concern.

During their long journey, they should have encountered other females and bulls in return with newly spawned hatchlings, but they did not meet another Ontaro. It had been a mystery to the herd, and they had learned the cruel reason for the absence of their kin in the last seconds of their life.

Huna pushed away from the hunters as hard as she could to drift alongside the rocks. Many hunters aimed and missed their target. She was soon out of the range of their weapons. However, she knew that she had to shed her outer shell on the rocks before seeking entry into the brown dwarf nursery.

The hunters did not make it easy for her to attempt entry into the old star, as she dodged countless harpoons and nets. She had to break the shell, so she ventured until she found a seemingly unpopulated rock and rubbed against it, shaking the asteroid violently. Inadvertently, she bounced several hunters from the rock, as Huna did not realize that the metal men were hiding in its crevices. Pieces of the shell broke off, at which point the hidden hunters on the rock took the chance to throw their harpoons into her vulnerable flesh. Most hunters leashed themselves to a harpoon line anchored to the asteroid. Chuk had not taken this precaution and was thus thrust into the black to drift eternal. His men bellowed their rage and concerns to their beloved leader as he helplessly floated off into the distance.

The other hunters set upon Huna. Two managed to leap onto her unprotected sections and stabbed unabated. She shook the men off and threw herself back into the dark. Unfortunately, the wounds she had received were deep and close to her heart, causing her to bleed profusely.

She sought a resting spot to recover her strength and attempt reentry, but she still had to shake the rest of the shell off or else fry up in the brown star. In search of a hiding space, she spotted a floating man. Despite her injuries, she swallowed the hunter and used her internal organs to place the unconscious Chuk into one of her sacs. Chuk was stirred awake by a resounding, gentle female voice.

"Hello! My name is Huna. I already know your name is Chuk and that you are a hunter. I found you in need of help and sacrificed one of my eggs to restore your health."

Chuk was vaguely aware of his surroundings in the sac of glowing energy, the fuzzy, solid state of static electricity. He felt invigorated and more alive than ever before. He understood what the creature was saying to him, even though his people only shared the limited communication of bellowing high to low-frequency pings to each other. It was thanks to

a telepathic link initiated by the Ontaro as he lay inside her organs.

"I hope you are feeling well and calm. I have a favor to ask of you."

"What you seek?" Chuk asked, sharing in Huna's telepathic link, albeit clumsily.

"I need help escorting my children home," replied Huna calmly. "I need to reach my ancestral birthing grounds to lay my eggs, but your people prevent it," she explained, increasing her empathic elements to influence Chuk toward her goal.

"Me in prey?" asked Chuk, now probing the slimy edges of the sac. "Me not in the great white. I fall in black."

"You are alive. I am dying. The wounds your hunters inflicted were deep. I am bleeding, and infection has set in."

"Me proud of rock eaters. Maybe kill you inside. You food, but you do me a favor, so how can you help?" offered Chuk. He was still unsure where he was, whether this was a test of Hyu, or how he would return home.

"How do I get past the rocks to Hyu?" Huna pleaded. "When we left for the great spawning, your hunters were not present in these rocks. The amber light still bears the mark of our ancestral home, and its energy courses in my veins."

"I may be a space Chuk, but me no understand you food."

"We are alike, you and I. We share the same ambitions to live peacefully and have children."

"Chuk no want more rock eaters. Spoil hunt." He was a simple man with simple desires, unmoved by her line of reasoning.

"If you want more Ontaro meat, then you need to let a few of us live and have babies." She hoped to be more direct work with the space caveman. Even if he didn't care about raising a family, he must care about his stomach.

"Ah! A small pod," replied Chuk. He and the others had been disappointed by the decreasing sizes of the last herds.

"Yes, small pod. I need your help in laying my eggs, one of which was used to keep you alive. I didn't need to save you, and I didn't have this plan in mind when I did. I just sensed someone in need of help. Please, help me in return."

Chuk beat his chest twice in appreciation. "Chuk has a life debt to you. No life debt for eggs."

"Hunt us in the future by letting some of us live today," implored a weakened Huna. "I tire and fear being tracked along the rocks by a large party. I will not have the energy to finish the journey to the star."

"Track to Hyu. Chuk help. Hide in black."

"I will do as you suggest. I am too far from any bright star to recharge my cells. I am getting weaker and may fail to stir during the next cycle."

She did not speak for the balance of the cycle. Chuk tried to relay ideas to her, but Huna's capacity to understand was diminishing quickly, fading along with her strength. She had only one last gasp for her passenger.

"Get my eggs to their home." And with that, the last Ontaro turned cold. The sac Chuk lay within began to lose its glow, and finally, it was completely dark.

Chuk was at a loss as to how he could help the Ontaro that saved him. He took stock of his skills and knowledge. He pondered how he could transport the eggs to Hyu, against the wishes of his people, who made it a point never to lose a target.

He felt guilt for the first time and channeled the confusing emotional energy to trying to resolve the life debt he owed. He could wait for Hyu's tides to pull him in, like all the other carcasses that eventually hit the rocks, but that would be far too slow; at that rate, the hunters would indeed find Huna's body and take her carcass and her eggs.

Chuk contemplated his fate long and hard. He had no tools or means to contact his tribe. His only relevant skill was dismembering the carcass and preparing it for market. He considered the properties of the Ontaro's skin and its conductive effects that the Kaku harnessed to their benefit in their space suits. The hunters did not have the language to describe the sophistication of the Ontaro's complex physiology—an ancient species that had roamed space for over a billion years—only the practical application of their carcasses to suit the metal men's needs.

Trapped in the interior of the rapidly rotting Ontaro, Chuk was spared the smell of Huna's bloody, decomposing body by having no olfactory senses. However, the space within the sac was empty of nourishment and short on elbow room. Chuk was feeling smothered and claustrophobic inside, and he sought an exit from the lifeless sac near the stomach.

The breathing tube extended from the crown, branching from the mouth, and the blow hole leading to the eggs typically regurgitated into a warm gas body through the female's mouth. The lungs and stomach connected to this breathing tube, so Chuk used this knowledge to plan his escape route.

The internal structure of the Ontaro's body was collapsing. The gas that filled the vacuum in the sac Chuk was residing in was now gone, and its walls began to press on him tightly. He slithered uncomfortably between the collapsed gas collectors and the lining of the stomach. It was an acid-free function that stored hydrogen gas to feed and nourish the egg sacs that were now starving. The other egg sacs were no longer glowing as brightly as before. He had to work quickly to get them home in time.

While slithering about on his belly, he found shards of rock and debris that Huna had sucked in with the gas. Chuk held up the sharpest stone and cut straight up from his location. He was familiar with Ontaro's anatomy, having butchered so many of them after hunts, and his family often used the blow hole equalizer as a quick entry to remove the egg sacs before the arrival of other greedy hunters who would take a stake in the kill by assisting in the division of the beast.

He had to find the clenched entry to the air tube. He found it hard to shuffle about underneath the crush of the lungs, so he had to act carefully. If he made the wrong cut, he would fill the interior with the creature's blood, and any attempt to navigate the internal organs would fail.

After hours of exhausting struggling, he found the tight knot of muscles he sought, which remained clasped shut. He carved around the bone into the cartilage of the gastric sphincter's base. The sharp rock performed its function well. The tube was now open, and Chuk entered. He made progress worming through the twelve-foot stomach tube, stopping when he reached the breathing chute and sliced it open.

Sticky mucus bands filled the long tube, stretched between the collapsing walls. Chuk was thankful that the thirty-foot climb would be made more accessible by the tube's natural ridges and structural folds. The thick mucus made the advancement slow and sticky, but the substance helped him hold onto the inner walls, and the internal hairs made ample rods for grabbing. He finally reached the blow hole and squeezed through the opening of the breathing tube to emerge outside the body, wholly filthy and covered in goop.

Chuk sat down heavily upon Huna's bloodstained back to wipe his face and rest his drained muscles from all the crawling, cutting, and climbing he had done for the past many hours. He surveyed the rocks of the icy belt that surrounded his home. He was sure his people were already cleaning their kills and celebrating the catch of the hunt with singing and feasting.

Swamped by doubt and guilt, he contemplated his loyalties and the old legends of how the hunters had migrated to the rocks of Hyu from across the blackness, guided by the stars and soaring on skin sails. The great Aptuk had led their tribe to Hyu from his sister Uyh by crossing the vast distance from their long abandoned home grounds near the dead giants. He watched the procession of the other hunters in the space, bellowed the ancient songs, and then danced the knowledge dance to divine his following path. His brain was on fire, and finally, he felt Hyu's divine answer for him.

"Aha! A sail!" bellowed Chuk.

He set about his task. He needed tools and a plan. He had no rope, fabric, or the traditional means to carve the bones. He studied the situation closely. At the very least, he would begin the dissection. The first cut was the most important. The mouth would be the starting place, and he crawled into position to find the best spot. He gripped his sharp rock and started his first cut with the curl at the corners of the mouth and slit the skin and fatty back. After scoring both ends, he sliced the dorsum until he had four front pieces. He pulled the skin to the posterior of the carcass and labored to separate the skin from muscle and fat to render the skin light and flexible.

Chuk left long tangles at the end of each section, which he would use to tie back the first parts of the sail. He had nothing to prop up the skin sail, but at least it was in position, and he ensured that the four sail points were firmly grounded in the flesh. He set aside the bounty of meat and fat and entered Huna's opened body to start gutting her, making sure to save long lengths of ligament and tendon to braid into ropes he would need. The work was filthy and exhausting, but he didn't stop. He continued in his labors, removing her flesh and organs until her carcass was like a hollow cavern. The dimly glowing egg sacs were the only contents left inside her body.

Chuk still needed to prop up the sail. He figured he could source the ribs and set about removing only every other bone, lest he risks instability in the body's skeletal frame. One rib after another was laboriously sawn at and wrenched out until he had four bones of approximately the same size. He set about planting the rib bones in the roof of the corpse and then slung the prepared skin over the bony frame. He worked on calibrating the fittings of the sails and then ventured proudly about his new sailing vessel, admiring his fine work, eventually settling himself down near the blow hole.

The hunter held four ropes, each tied to a corner of the unfurled sail. Immediately unfolding, he felt a light push as the skin reacted to the amber starlight. Absorption of the photons caused the makeshift craft to trudge forward as it slowly gained momentum due to the coherence properties of the Ontaro membrane. As he steered his new vessel, Chuk hoped that the sail he created would get them to move fast enough.

The inner rocks were soon within view, and the sight of the strange, mutilated Ontaro stirred excitement within the tribe. The hunters were eager to make up for the dismal haul this past migration, and Chuk was sure that was what the tribe members planned on doing while waiting on the rocks ahead. He knew of the few places where the stones were too far apart and too chaotic for the hunters to roam. He had to head there for any chance of reaching Hyu.

Chuk's approach to the belt was reasonably fast but still too slow to evade the hunters. He spotted the other hunters bouncing about the rocks in pursuit. Amused by the grotesque construct, they wondered if they saw a mirage or vision. They spoke to one another of the hunter riding the Ontaro canoe, like in the old tales told during feasts.

It looked as if Chuk was parading the corpse for his fellow hunters to view when he pursued the hollow space and hoped to lose the hunting procession that followed him. Chuk had little choice but to plod along at this rate of speed. He expected their harpoons to latch onto Huna's body at any moment when he suddenly had an idea.

Chuk dumped the loads of butchered meat and internal organs he had separated earlier in hopes of lightening the load and speeding up his flight. He slung the valuable cargo towards the rocks with a mighty effort from his tired arms. He hoped his aim was accurate so the bounty would not drift into the rainbow darkness. The meat hit the magic spot, and the other hunters danced their praise.

However, the closer he got to Hyu's rocky belt, the more the bellows echoed off his skin. Their excitement soon became cries of concern as they wondered why he had not yet beached the Ontaro's carcass. No hunter's bellow yet bore his name, which Chuk was relieved to find, as this meant that his clan was innocent of his treacherous action.

He tossed the last sacs of meat and fat as he passed the primary rock, praying for redemption. The eggs began to liven in their glow as if already tasting the hot gases of the star. He was now directly adjacent to "Hyu's Teeth," the ominous landmark of his trek's final hurdle.

The Ontaro canoe gained in speed as Chuk neared the hollow space. The dwarf was feeding the approach with the increasing pull of its gravity. The hunters followed Chuk with angry bellows that bounced off his back. They did not understand his irrational maneuver and sought to stop him. The hunters who pursued him knew of the honors that awaited them if they caught this errant Ontaro. Chuk understood this and ignored the bellows, continuing on his destined course. He concentrated on entering the hollow—somewhere other hunters feared to venture—into Hyu's embrace, welcoming him as a swirling vortex of razor-sharp shards making up a chaotic mouth.

Chuk slunk down into the blow hole of the corpse, shielding himself from Hyu's biting rocky teeth. He blindly steered as the sail was shredded and became useless. The sharp pebbles nibbled at the canoe inch by inch, stripping the last of Huna's bone and flesh. At last, he was naked before his god. He wore a smile in offering to the brown dwarf.

"Hyu, embrace me. I come home to the white."

THE ENDLESS STAIRCASE

THE MACHINE was in recycle mode. the rider and the man watched as the last photon gasped, and the universe went dark. The expansive prison had no walls. His only chains were his form being separated atom by atom and his bio-signature stripped from the particles that once bore his shape and were no longer loyal to signatures born in the furnaces of stars as they were stripped of their electrons and dissipated. They were the only witnesses to the end of time—when light gave way to darkness, and quarks rendered dissolved in the endless, boundless edges of this subverse.

The pair and the 'next to last particle out' were drawn to the gulf. The lull of an epic nap to the end of the universe was the only ticket out of the sublime.

"Those Ontaro. The last life form to scurry between galaxies, now too epic in scale to make the journey hardly worth the effort. Their journey ends as the last sparks of the machine fade. They think they are the subject of the universe's abstract expressionistic character study, much like you think I am here because you misrecognize the situation, you phallo-logocentric freak."

"I am just as confused as when I arrived. If anything, I suspect you have lesions on the brain," grumbled the man. "Phallo, what?"

"You speak the truth regarding confusion. There is no lesson. I took liberties by taking you on a fast-forward trip along the arrow of time. We skipped through dead people's lives and had a blast!"

"To what end? Why me?" responded the man.

"Why not you? I hijack souls in passage to other lives and ride the only construct other than entropy that has any use for time. I ride herd over the planes of existence by pulling back the cheeks of your bally face and spurring you forward."

"I am your beast of burden! A horse?" intoned the man.

"I normally just let them go after one use...but you, I like. You remind me of myself a few incarnations back."

"Take me back now!" demanded the man.

"Although the universe is a stack of possibilities, the gap of probable outcomes plastered by the reserves of the failed universes dictates that your request requires a journey from the beginning to the end of time for each incarnation of the machine is required to squander their reserve, to achieve utter dissipation and restart the cycle. While parallel existences run counter to each other, and each second forward slathered on a future or a past already consummated in tandem with other subverses that we experience as Déjà Vu—It eliminates those excess moments we all share across incarnations—and frankly, your minute has passed."

"WHAT," shouted the man in their weird space, "is the point of all this?"

"How much more deconstruction? There is no metaphysical point! I just needed a ride out of this universe. You were dying, and the machine was opening, and well, I seized the 10^{-43}."

"You have to be zorking kidding me. Take me back," the bitter man said. "I have a family."

"You also have a drinking problem. You expired, you turd." The being was still in good spirits. He enjoyed the banter. "Maybe I need to rephrase this. Your other incarnations got it. There is no going back in time unless you have the power of all the universes at your disposal. The only residual of time is memory; the remaining energy balances an infinite stack of pancakes, and as it passes along, the only dynamic making the present possible is the redistribution of the past to seed the future. Witness your soul stretched across the spectrum of fractionalized possibilities that exist. Now, like me, you swim the mists of time, freed of the confines of matter and stripped to the most basic particle with no spin or mass. The soul boson. The witness state of the neutrinos. The symmetry assassin."

"I am completely lost now," spoke the defeated man.

"It's all in the pursuit of adding a little old jouissance magic to your existence, being rocked by the unknown. But you failed to frame your past life properly and sought extreme pleasure. In your hysteria, you tasted extreme displeasure in return, and you wonder why me. For me, I seek the exit. But it is not for you. Your thoughts are your only mass. Your drive, spin, and residue is the symmetry assassin I speak of."

The gulf was signaling the end of its cycle. It awaited one last soul to spark the reset. All were stuck in a state of flux until called on.

"Come," cooed a trillion voices. "Join us. Time to recycle."

"I'm going to the party over there. Before I leave, I have a bit of wisdom for you. Parallel universes exist beside each other, but time runs in opposite directions. You are the plus one in this egg; you will exist but not live; the park is now yours, and your surroundings will begin to make sense," the being said as the gulf closed.

The man was alone in his austere and somber cell. The Jouissance the being spoke of worked her doubled-sided nature, and the eruptive exuberant emotions gave way to melancholy and suffering. Without conversation, he worked to hold his ties to the old world. He was Seru Pho. He had a wife, a kid, and two years of service left on the icy moon before redeployment. He remembered that together, they had a vested hope that the rotation would change the environment that had poisoned their relationship.

The bitterness returned to him. He remembered that as the monotonous rhythm set in, so did cabin fever and the ongoing inebriation. The replicator churning out cold scotch gas and the occasional chickpea pretzel. Only now does the man realize the stupor he was in and that his wife took to her lab to avoid him as his mood swings left the situation to be what it was. He ignored that his wife theorized that the varying levels of gravity would alter the human's brain chemistry. In her feasibility analysis on Saturn, she stated that conditions similar to Mercury's madness would arise, and she was sure Saturn's tidal influence had set upon him. A neuron here, a neuron there, and a polarizing personality change would emerge akin to Dr. Jekyll and Mr. Hyde. He heartily denied any validity to her accusations during their many fights. He regretted that he did not listen to her.

His thoughts of her—as unsettled and riddled with guilt as they were—still comforted him as he drifted in the null. He repeatedly repeated the same stories to himself in his dark cell and muttered about the cruel design. His form was neutral and unbound, and his instinct gave over to awareness as his bonds became visible, making his escape questionable. He could discern interlocking links of dimensional foam but no color, light, sound, or pressure.

The machine reset over eternity as the dérive spirit of his existence bobbed the man along to observe the forces that held him at bay in this strange cell. Energy throbbing at low levels and an eternity of observation led him to theorize that he was of vast power in limited supply spread wide distribution. This space dispersed his essence into other dimensions, similar to the pinpoints and balls he observed when he first met the being. His current position was the backside of god, for before him was a pinpoint of extreme mass, temperature,

and density. Black holes from other universes collected matter and energy that filtered into his space as unformed pre-elements. The machine's skin grew tighter as failed universes squeezed into the collection point.

He felt in awe as the machine's inner workings revealed its détournementing nature to him freely. The void was small; only the canvas was yet another chora, and he was the smallest element in this space. He watched as the void lit up with beaded filaments that formed the outer shell filled with time's spent rounds of cosmic background radiation, serving its eternal sentence of dissipation and ambiance to support a pastiched under rigging. Only his consciousness held the balance between the push and pull of the two and maintained the structural integrity of his growing form. The vacuum filled with cosmic junk as the man pushed through the clinched tight anus of the multi-universe. The subverse's balance was off due to the man's presence. Instead of dissipation in the arena of plus and minus, he thrust forward into the inferno undergoing rapid inflation.

The man finally settled in a cloud of gas bonded to a hydrogen atom. He resided for eons in the cold cell as it congealed into heavy packs that sparked the birth of the first stars. The immense pressure went unnoticed by the man, but the emergence of a super gigantic red star beyond comprehension in proportions of the first-generation stars did not.

The star had a sister, which was consuming its sibling. The man's stay in the gigantic star was brief before being transferred to the vicious little star in a plasma stream. He was transformed and stepped up the periodic table until his soul boson fused with an iron atom. His expulsion from the dying star into the darkness shattered his tranquil existence, where he floated for an eternity, gathering dust and clumping with other matter.

For billions of years, he circled a young yellow star. Gravity pulled him onto the third rock to the next epoch in his life. He was under constant transformation. His earliest memory of the planet was fire, then the water. His iron atom was eventually freed from its prison of conversion, only to be laid upon by a single-celled creature. He suffered the indignity of being digested for fuel before expulsion from the rear of the bacteria. His brief yet destructive stay threw him back to the mercy of the acidic water and set the tone for the next stage of his life.

His iron atom-shell oxidized into expressions of fractured memes aped by other atoms. His soul muon held to the nucleus. He drifted in his existence as a free atom, collecting and discarding electrons at a whim until one day, lichen grasped his structure, and he was held hostage to a granite rock for millennia.

Time was only measured when the man was part of a living system. As life evolved, so did his cage. From a frog swallowed by a bird to a deer killed by a wolf, the man trickled in and out of a cycle of flesh and excrement, traveling up and down the digestive tracks from animal to insect to microbe and back up again. His final phase was as objects fashioned from iron. He fought in battles as a weapon and flew into space as a bolt.

Eventually, the spacecraft—his residence—was scrapped, and he was recycled and ground up as an iron supplement for vitamins. He soon found himself riding shotgun on a chickpea pretzel, entering the cycle of consumption that he was all too familiar with. As he hit the stomach, something nagged at him.

In the digestive pit, the pretzel he hitched a ride on dissolved, and he was absorbed into a slurry of the four stomachs. A green blood cell floated by and seized his iron atom.

"I bet you didn't think you would hear from me again," spoke the being that was the green blood cell. "Our journey will be complete with your muon in place."

The kidnapper instinctively headed to the sector of the biological construct where the soul muon receptor lay in a loose synapse plug. The body stirred. Its death throes shook the pair. The being drove the blood cell to its final destination to beat the clock running out. In a blink, the race was over.

The man found himself in a weird expression of his old domicile on Titan. His vaguely familiar wife and kid sat before him, concerned. Tears flowed from many unmatched tentacle eyes that dripped blue drops on their synthetic chaps. The man blinked his eyes and rubbed the many extensions of sight but did not have enough hands to clear the gunk that blurred his vision.

"We jump the tracks now," said the being faintly in the back of his mind, "Hold on, my old friend, in a snap, I return you to your fate at the crossroads of Déjà Vu. Seize your bliss, for it will not last before we journey to stir the dreamer from its 16 billion-year nap and save the metaverse from collapse."

His existence blinked. His mind was blank, and it was dark. A flicker of light breached the darkness as his eyelids separated. Before him, his concerned wife and child were crying. He pulled them into his arms and never let go.

THE BEGINNING

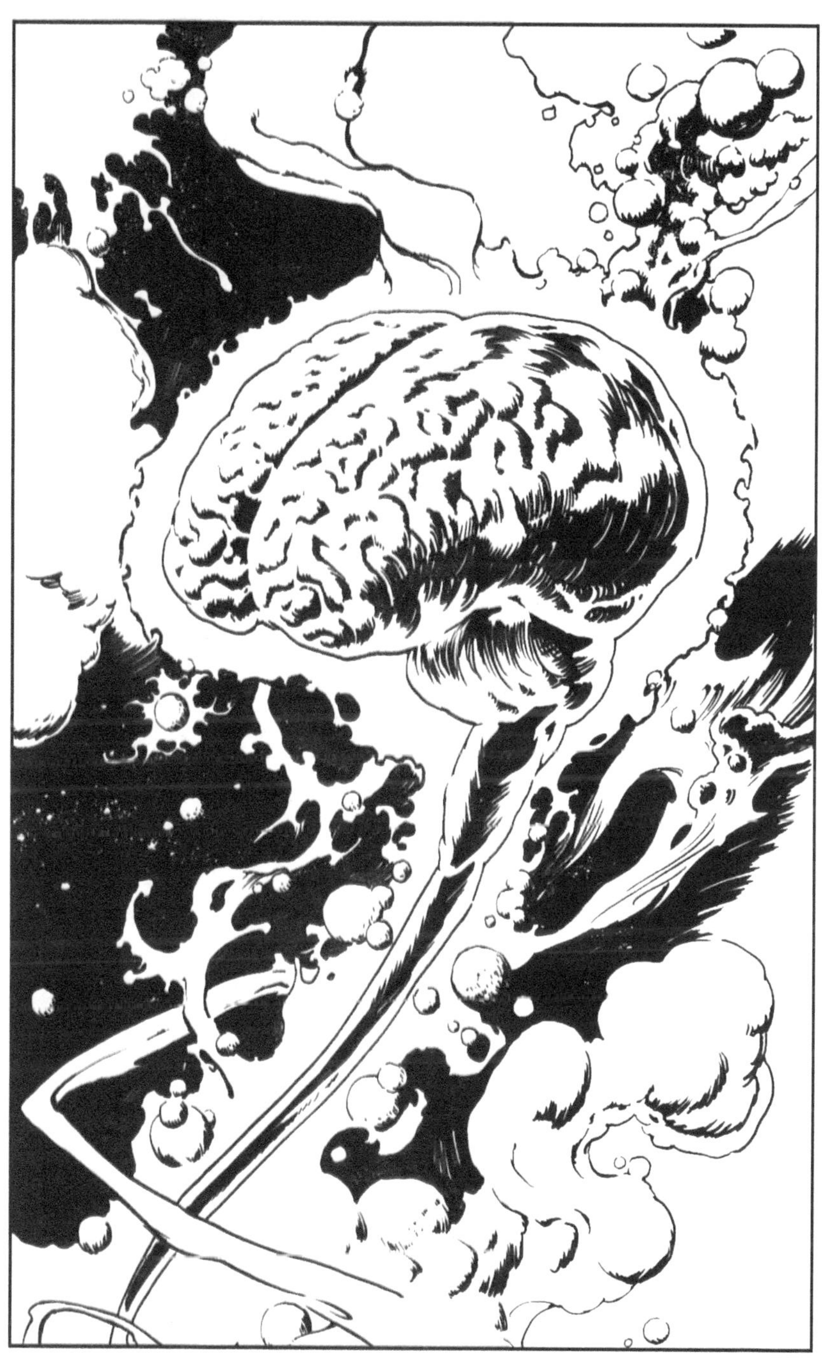

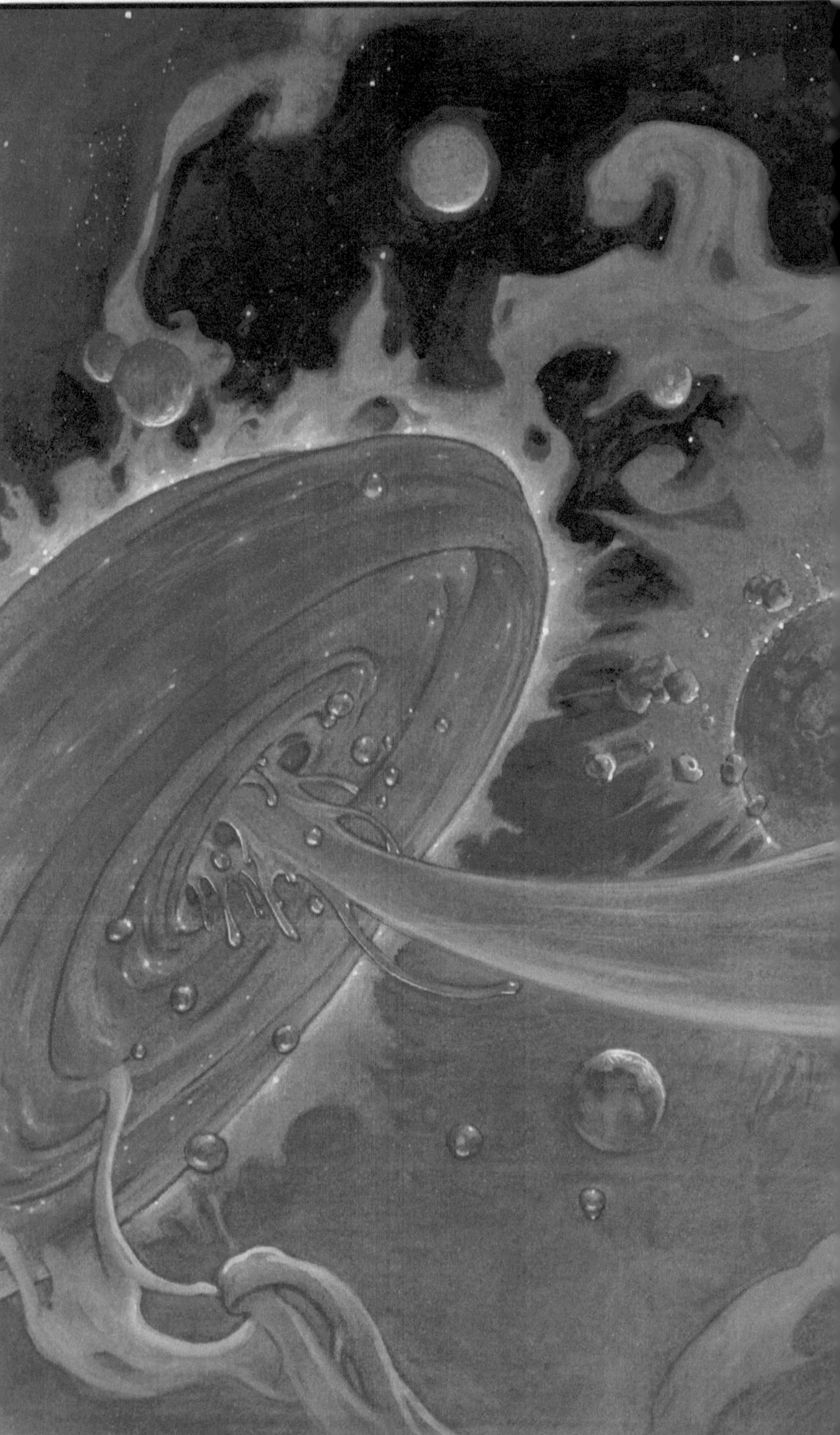

ODDNESS

This reclusive person (author, publisher, producer, editor) specializes in crafting captivating short story collections, novellas, and comics that transport readers to extraordinary realms is also the driving force behind Forbidden Futures magazine, where the fantastic and the unbelievable come to life.

Originating from unknown lands, ODDNESS dabbles in composing electronic music and playing video games.

MIKE DUBISCH

This graphic novelist and illustrator has been creating and publishing comics and art since the 1980s. He has carved out a unique place creating horror, science-fiction, surrealism, and YA adventure works using all but lost traditional techniques. Born in California, USA, the artist has traveled and lived in five countries. He has been an instructor at the Academy Of Art University since 2012 and is married to children's book illustrator and sculptor Carolyn Watson Dubisch, with whom he has three daughters.

FUTURES

www.ingramcontent.com/pod-product-compliance
Lightning Source LLC
Chambersburg PA
CBHW030336310726
48979CB00001B/63

* 9 7 8 1 9 6 0 2 1 3 3 3 4 *